D1302963

About the Illustrator

Name: ....

Age: .... Hometown: ....

The craziest thing I've ever done is:

....

My favorite dinner is: ....

I wish the world was made out of this type of food:

....

Our Crazy Dinner

COMPENDIUM®

kids™

inspiring possibilities.™

We sat down at the table
like we always do, but dinner

at my house tonight wasn't like
anything I've ever seen before.

First, the broccoli started to grow and grow, taller and taller and taller, until the stalks looked like trees over our heads.

We stood up from the table and started walking through the broccoli forest when we noticed that something was happening with the spaghetti.

I was swinging and higher and higher, swinging,

when the glasses of milk
spilled and started to spread.

Soon, the milk was a big white river, and we all jumped off the swings into the cool waves.

We swam and splashed and blew bubbles and suddenly I noticed

that the chocolate chip cookies
on the shore were getting larger.

"Cookie rafts!" I shouted and I dashed out of the milk river to grab a giant cookie. I rolled it down to the water and jumped on top of it. It floated perfectly.

Everyone else grabbed a cookie, too, and we raced down the river, paddling

with our hands and nibbling
on the chocolate chips.

We knew it was time for bed
when the napkins grew bigger

than blankets and soaked up
the whole river of milk.

I can't wait to see what we're having for breakfast!

WITH SPECIAL THANKS TO THE
ENTIRE COMPENDIUM FAMILY.

CREDITS:

Written by: M.H. Clark
Designed by: Julie Flahiff
Edited by: Amelia Riedler

ISBN: 978-1-935414-97-1

© 2013 by Compendium, Inc. All rights reserved. No part of this publication may be reproduced or transmitted in any form or by any means, electronic or mechanical, including photocopy, recording, or any storage and retrieval system now known or to be invented without written permission from the publisher. Contact: Compendium, Inc., 2100 North Pacific Street, Seattle, WA 98103. *Our Crazy Dinner*; *Story Lines*; Compendium; live inspired; and the format, design, layout, and coloring used in this book are trademarks and/or trade dress of Compendium, Inc. This book may be ordered directly from the publisher, but please try your local bookstore first. Call us at 800.91.IDEAS or come see our full line of inspiring products at live-inspired.com.

1st printing. Printed in China with soy inks. A0113030017500

COMPENDIUM®

kids™

inspiring possibilities.™